FEAR
and
FANTASY

PALMETTO
P U B L I S H I N G
Charleston, SC
www.PalmettoPublishing.com

Copyright © 2024 by Thomas Hughes

All rights reserved

No portion of this book may be reproduced, stored in a retrieval system, or transmitted in any form by any means– electronic, mechanical, photocopy, recording, or other– except for brief quotations in printed reviews, without prior permission of the author.

Paperback ISBN: 979-8-8229-4661-3

FEAR
and
FANTASY

*A Collection of Shorts and Poetry
inspired by my travels*

THOMAS HUGHES

CONTENTS

PART 1 FEAR 1
foreign deceiver 2
it hides, it lurks 3
blackened man 4
there stood a rich man 5
the town race 6
enter the alpha 9
the honey-do list 18
river bank nightmare 22

PART 2 FANTASY 41
somehow 42
path of the sun 43
working hands 48
harry and the sun fairy 61

PART I
FEAR

FOREIGN DECEIVER

A man came to a town from a foreign land.

A promise of goodness was enclosed in his hand.

When he opened his hand, all that was found

Was contempt and bitterness as it fell to the ground.

He promised prosperity and progress in whole,

But these things would cost them a piece of their soul.

The town, in their eagerness, had forgotten just this—

That a hand grasping a gift, still makes a fist.

IT HIDES, IT LURKS

It hides, it lurks,
It waits for me
Under a rock
Or in a tree.
It hides, it lurks,
It waits for me
Of all the others
It can see.
It hides, it lurks,
It waits for me;
I ask myself,
How can it be?
It hides, it lurks,
It waits for me;
Day in and out,
How I see.
It hides, it lurks,
It waits for me…

BLACKENED MAN

In my view beyond the tree,
The blackened man is watching me.
The things I've done, he can see.
He judges and waits so patiently.
It matters not how far I flee,
He's always just beyond the tree
To stake his claim eventually;
This blackened man that I can see.

THERE STOOD A RICH MAN

There stood a rich man high on his hill,

Using power of wealth to enforce his will.

He caused others to fall and looked down on them still.

They watched from below as the rich man grew ill,

Their knives at the ready as he fell from his hill.

THE TOWN RACE

He pedaled his bike as fast as he could. There was a hill coming up, and he needed all of the momentum that he could get to make it to the top and across the finish line. This was the first year that he was old enough to enter the big bicycle race that his town had held every year for the past twenty years. He'd spent his entire fifteenth year building his bike from spare parts that his father would find in various places, and exercising and riding across every type of terrain that his town had to offer, and it had paid off for him so far. He had not even felt any of the other racers even close to him since they'd all taken off from the starting line. The breeze created from his self-made pedal-speed was cooling the sweat that had escaped from his brow and slowly made its way down his face. This was a needed feeling, as he was beginning to fatigue a great deal from the uphill climb. Just a few more yards to go, and then he would just have the one hundred meters of downhill slope to get him across the finish line.

    He was close to the top of the hill when he felt a sharp pain shoot up the calf of his right leg. It was a cramp like he had never felt before, and it couldn't have come at a worse time. He had the option to stop and try to stretch out his leg, but he wasn't sure how far behind the others were, and he didn't want to risk being caught. He continued to pedal and the pain began to extend from his calf to just above his knee.

The pain was unbearable, but he managed to clear the top of the hill and coasted a bit to start his downhill ride. He straightened his right leg to the side to reduce the cramping effect. His ease would be short-lived, as he heard sounds closing in on him. He shook his foot and pedaled as hard as he could to increase his downhill speed. He could see the finish line more clearly now, maybe only thirty more meters to go. He was moving fast as the wind pushed his hair back; twenty more meters and victory was his.

Then came a metallic crunch at his feet, and suddenly his pedals were useless. His chain had broken. The only thought that entered his mind was to lower his head and upper body to reduce wind resistance and hope he still had enough speed built up to win. He sped across the finish line and had just enough space to stop before crashing into the gate at the finish line area. He stood to his feet, exhausted and thirsty.One of the aids handed him water as he watched the big metal gate close at the finish line, and at the same time, a big hairy creature that looked like a dog with the feet of a tiger and boar's tusks protruding from its mouth, slammed head first into the finish line gate.He looked toward a big screen to his right that had displayed the pictures of that day's racers.All of the faces except his were marked with red Xs. Not only was he the winner of today's race, but he was also the only survivor.

ENTER THE ALPHA

It took Ed a few minutes to clear the cobwebs from his mind, plus another minute or two for his vision to clear up. He had never driven in this much snow before. When the road had disappeared beneath a heavy white blanket of it, it had taken maybe five seconds for his car to leave the road and head into a ditch that had become hidden by the layer of white powder that had been falling for the past few hours. Before Ed had realized what had happened, his car had come to a sudden stop at the bottom of the ditch, and his forehead had slammed into the steering wheel. He cleared his mind up as much as possible, given the circumstances of the past few minutes, and put on his jacket to step out into the sharp five-degree weather that awaited him outside of his car.

Ed checked his watch, which now displayed 2:45 p.m. In this part of the world, that meant he had about an hour before it was dark out. He never could get used to these Eastern European winters and their shorter than usual days. He knew that there was slim to zero chance of getting his car out before the next day, and there was an even slimmer chance of anyone passing by to offer him a ride. No locals were foolish enough to go driving on a snow-blanketed road at this hour of the day. His cell phone was no use either, as there was zilch service due to the storm and his remote location. Yep, Ed knew he had only one option for help, and that option was his own two feet. He also knew that he'd better put that option to work quickly, because once it got dark, the temperature was going to drop about another ten to twenty degrees outside. He remembered passing a small wood barn about a mile back that sat about a half mile off the road. Ed grabbed a flashlight from his trunk, locked his doors, and headed back into the flurry of early-evening snow.

The wood barn appeared in his view just as the sun was about even with the tree line behind him. He didn't see any sort of road or driveway that led to the barn, which meant it was most likely accessible from the other side, but that also meant that just beyond the barn, there might be a house and someone that could at least give him a ride or let him use the phone to call for a ride. As much as he hated the idea of trudging across a snow-covered field that most likely contained a nice soft layer of field mud mixed beneath that layer of cold, deep snow, he hated the idea of being outdoors in subzero weather even more; so across the field it was. He grumbled under his breath as he stepped onto the field. If Ed's eyes hadn't been so focused on the wood barn across the field, maybe he would have looked to his right and possibly caught a glimpse of the big pair of pale-amber eyes that watched him from just behind the tree line.

The first few steps went along easily enough. It wasn't until Ed was about fifty paces in that his foot really sank through the cold snow and into the damp earth that was beneath. "Out here freezing my skin off and almost losing my shoes in the muck," he grumbled to himself. As tried to shake a bit of wet dirt from his shoe, the pair of eyes shifted from the tree line and slowly but quietly began to move along the field. The eyes belonged to a wolf—a very hungry wolf at that.

Ed had given up on trying to remove all of the muck from his shoe and resumed his trek across the field; still unaware of his hungry pursuer. He was about to curse the weather, snow, and mud once more, but his words were brought to a halt in his throat as he glanced toward the tree line to his right. A wolf had popped its head from the trees to peer at Ed as saliva dripped from its jaws. It wasn't until he turned to survey the left tree line for a possible escape that he saw the first wolf that had been stalking him the moment he stepped onto the field. Ed stood there for a moment, partially paralyzed in fear and partially contemplating his next move.

He was way too far from the barn to make a run for it, plus the field would definitely make running an impossibility. He had heard somewhere that most domestic dogs would chase you if you ran, but he wasn't sure if that applied to wolves. Standing here any longer was no smart option either. The sun was setting, and if the wolves didn't get him, the subzero weather was bound to. Ed kept his head slightly lowered and walked at a snail's pace toward the old wood barn. "Maybe there's an axe in the barn, or perhaps something to make a fire with," he thought to himself. He had heard somewhere that wolves didn't like fire. He ran these thoughts through his mind and continued slowly. The wolves followed at a matching pace but made no effort to gain ground on Ed.

Ed managed to keep both predators in his side views but made no sudden glances in either direction to avoid quick movements. Ed was only about fifty feet from the barn. He waited for the feeling of sharp teeth sinking into his leg or maybe the back of his neck, but felt neither. The only thing he felt was a small glimmer of hope as the ground beneath his feet became solid. He was finally out of the field and back on solid ground.That's when the burst of desperation hit him—both wolves immediately went from a slow trot to a full run in pursuit ofEd.Ed also went into a full-on run toward his only hope of sanctuary.It was only another twenty-five feet to the barn and then around to the side to find the door.Twenty-five feet, twenty, fifteen, ten, five…

There was a blinding pain in Ed's right calf as he fell to his stomach. One of the wolves, the second wolf, had caught up and sank its teeth into his lower leg as it dragged him to the ground.Ed's hands scrambled all around him on the ground, looking for something, anything, he could use as a weapon to break the vice grip of teeth from his leg.All he found was earth for a few seconds, and then, just before the other wolf could join in for the kill bite on Ed's throat, his hand hit something solid—an axe handle that was lying beside the old barn. He could tell that the head was missing by the weight of it, but the broken end worked just fine and found its mark as Ed sunk it into the eye of his attacker. A high pitched yelp escaped the beast's mouth as it released its grip and staggered backward, shaking its head.

The original wolf had just reached them, but it stopped immediately and began a slow walk toward Ed while growling slowly. Ed had now regained his vertical base and was leaning against the side of the barn with the broken axe held out in front of him like a spear to ward off both wolves. He slowly backed around the edge of the barn with his free hand feeling the way behind him while also using the barn like a crutch to take the weight of his mangled leg. As Ed reached the corner of the barn, he reached his hand around and felt not a door but an opening. He took his chance, and lunged for the opening, hoping for his life that a door would be there to close out the hungry beasts.

And there was a door! "Thank God!" he said as he attempted to slam it closed. A wolf rammed into the door just before it closed and caused Ed to lose balance and fall to a seated position. Its head was just inside the door as Ed used his good leg to kick the door closed and hold the wolf's head in place. He stabbed the axe handle point into the hungry creature's upper snout, which caused it to yelp and pull its head back out of the door. Ed managed to return to his feet and brace his body weight against the door while looking for a latch, lock, or anything else that could keep the door closed. He found nothing but braces on each side of the door that looked like they could hold a board or plank across the door to keep it closed. He had nothing to put across the door. Nothing except his axe handle. He placed the handle on the braces on either side and just hoped that it would hold them. There were a few more bumps against the door, a few growls, and then silence.

The sun had set and the inside of the barn was now as dark as the outside. Ed stood by the door for a few more seconds, to be sure that his attackers had relented, before he turned his back to the door to search for a light switch or at least a lantern. He stepped back a few feet from the door, never completely turning his back to it, and felt along the wall. "Yes!' he said as his hand landed on something familiar—a light switch! Ed flipped the switch, and for a brief moment, his heart leaped as the room lit up, but it sank immediately as the bulb flickered and lowered tremendously. The low flickering produced just enough light for Ed to make out a few vague shapes and nothing more. He attempted to pivot away from the door, but not without checking first to make sure it was still secure with the old axe handle. His attempt was met with failure as a sharp pain, from the mangled flesh that was once his calf, shot up his calf to the back of his upper leg. He immediately lost his balance and fell, face first, to the earthen floor of the old wood barn. He lay there facedown for a few minutes until the burning pain subsided just a bit. He decided that maybe crawling would be a better means of exploring the semi-darkened shed. The last thing he needed was to stumble around and fall on a hay fork or an upturned hay hook. Perhaps there was a ladder that led to the loft, and he could manage a climb to secure a bit more safety from his current situation.

He crawled forward, slowly, for about five feet and found not a ladder but a set of furry claws attached to yet another growling wolf. He froze in place, paralyzed in fear as he turned his head a bit to the right. The flicker of low light allowed Ed to catch a glimpse of falling saliva as it dripped from the monster's teeth and landed on the dirt floor beside Ed's right hand. Another flicker of light cast a brief shadow on the wall in the direction in which Ed was looking; a shadow of a figure that was twice the size of the two that were pacing the barn's outside perimeter. Yet another flicker and he saw the dirt at the base of the barn door was beginning to move from the outside as the other two wolves began to dig their way to the meal that now bowed at the front paws of their alpha wolf.

Ed had barely closed his eyes to say a prayer when the blinding stab of four big canines pierced the back of his skull, causing him to fall flat on his stomach and gasp inward with pain, sucking dirt into his mouth as he did. The flickers of light now became red flashes as blood filled Ed's eyes. He could feel the teeth release their grasp from his skull. He watched, almost paralyzed with shock from the pain, as one wolf's head entered from outside through the freshly dug hole; then a second wolf followed. Ed tried to focus on the wounded eye of the wolf that had attacked his leg earlier, but only caught a glimpse of the eight paws that now stood to his right. That was the last thing that Ed saw as the alpha once more lunged down with its sharp teeth and mighty jaws, this time almost completely engulfing Ed's neck. There was a sharp pain at the top of his spine followed by a snap of vertebrae being twisted and then crushed. Then there was nothing as the two smaller wolves waited for their share of the meal as the alpha began to eat.

THE HONEY-DO LIST

Mow the lawn—check. Repair the back doorknob—check. Install those shelves in the closet—check. Place the trash bin on the curb for pick up—check.

Only two more items remained on Scott's self-made honey-do list, and these were probably the most important. Scott had to pick up his wife's gift from the jeweler and stop by the local vineyard to get her favorite bottle of wine. You see, this was no ordinary Friday for Scott. This Friday was special for two reasons. It was his first day off in his much-needed two-week vacation—he had just finished a project for his company. This was a project that had demanded almost two whole months of working every day; two whole months of missed dinners, neglected house chores and a neglected wife. His wife, who had pretty much run their relationship from date number one, had been very bitter and vocal for the entire two months. She was quick to remind him of his missed home chores, his missed date nights, and many other things. It didn't matter that he had worked his way through college, while supporting them both, to obtain his civil engineering degree. It didn't matter that within his fifth year with the company, he had already been appointed as the head of city planning and design. It didn't' matter that his first major assignment was overseeing the planning and building of the community's first-ever assisted-living neighborhood, which would house over five hundred elderly, disabled, or retied people. It also didn't matter to Scott how much she complained. He loved his wife and his job. Through the entire two months, no matter how tired he was or how many complaints he got from home, all that he thought about was how many people he would help with this project and how much he was going to make the missed time up to his wife.

This brings us to the second and most important reason that this Friday was special. Today was his five-year wedding anniversary. Nothing would dampen his mood today. He finally had two weeks to repay his wife for all of the lost time and neglect.

Pick up wife's new necklace from jewelers—check. Pick up her favorite bottle of wine from the vineyard—check.

The only thing that felt bigger than his pride from his finished list was the warm feeling from his heart about the upcoming evening. He couldn't wait to sneak into their bedroom and place the wine and necklace on her bedside table without waking her. She most likely would still be asleep when he arrived. He knew this from her voice message the previous day: "It's me. I made dinner for myself. You can grab something for yourself on the way home since you care about those old drains on society more than your wife. Just go ahead and crash on the couch when you get home. I need the sleep, so I'm gonna take a valium, and I don't really feel like being woken up when you come in so late."

Scott hadn't received a call from home the entire morning, which meant that his secret plan was working. This made him feel ever happier as he slowly unlocked his front door. He eased it open and stepped inside quietly. He made his way down the main hall and stopped at the kitchen to get two wine glasses and a corkscrew. He slowly pushed open their bedroom door and poked his head in. Sure enough; she lay quietly on her side in the bed. She was facing her bedside table and was unmoved by his slight noise of him stepping inside.

He moved around the room to her side of the bed and lightly placed the bottle, bottle opener, glasses, and the small box containing her gift on her bedside table. He smoothly opened the bottle, once again without disturbing his wife. This made him think to himself and smile a bit. "Scott, you sneaky fellow."

He poured each glass about half full and set the bottle down. She did not stir even a bit as he took his glass of wine and kissed her cheek ever so lightly. He whispered into her ear, "Don't worry, my dear. Things will be so different now. I hope you like the things I have done around the house today. I love you so much. I promise that you will never have to complain to me ever again. This is going to be such a great day for us. I just wish to say happy anniversary to you, my beautiful wife."

He gently touched her forehead and used his middle and forefinger to close her dead but open eyes before he left the room. He turned out the light and closed the door. His wife lay motionless and lifeless on her side. The bruise around her neck had grown more dark and profound since the previous night, especially the two thumb-shaped bruises that met near the center of the throat. These were almost the same size and shape of her loving husband's thumbs...

RIVER BANK NIGHTMARE

It was 2:55 p.m. on a late spring day in 1990. The last five minutes of Kyle's school day seemed to take hours to pass by. This wasn't just a normal 3:00 p.m. that he was waiting for. It was 2:55 p.m. on a Friday, but not just any Friday. This was the last Friday of the last day of his sixth-grade school year. Just five measly minutes stood between him and three months of freedom—three months of swimming, cookouts, fishing, no homework, and all other things that most twelve-year-olds hold at high importance. Five minutes! He was sitting on his hands in anticipation. Five of the slowest minutes he had ever encountered seemed more like it.

He wasn't alone in his impatience. His best friend Jamie was counting the minutes with him. You see, tonight wasn't just the start of their summer break. It was also their first unsupervised camping trip to their favorite hangout spot on the river. It had taken them the past month to not only gather supplies but, more importantly, to convince their parents that they were both mature and responsible enough to handle a weekend on the river without any parents around. With the help of a few classes at the local game-warden station on survival, first aid, and campfire safety, both sets of parents agreed.

Just when both boys thought that they could no longer stand the waiting, 2:59, by some miracle it seemed, became 3:00, and that final school bell had never sounded so great!

Jamie and Kyle raced down the hall as fast as they could. They saw Jamie's dad parked out front in his truck, but the truck wasn't what they both focused on. It was the small canoe that sat on the trailer connected to the truck and the two full packs of camping gear that sat in the truck bed that had their attention. One bag held their two-man tent that they had found at an old army-supply store in town, and the other held their survival gear that included a first-aid kit, waterproof matches, a hatchet for firewood, and a machete for brush. There were also two small sets of fishing tackle to use to catch their dinner and a few cans of Vienna sausages and saltine crackers in case the fish weren't biting.

Jamie's dad dropped them off at a small river-landing, wished them good luck, and reminded them to be safe. It was only about a mile of paddling up the river to their favorite hangout spot beside the riverbank. They had spent a great deal of their weekends during the school year cleaning out heavy brush and making a decent firepit from bigger rocks they had found along the banks. They had even managed to find, cut, and stack a decent-sized pile of firewood. They had all that they needed, and everything seemed all set for a guy's weekend on the river.

They were about half a mile from their landing spot when Kyle took his small portable FM radio from his pack and put on some music for their short but tiring journey upstream against the current. The music was just a short-lived welcome against the quiet before that dreaded "Now a word from out sponsors…" played as the song ended. Jamie rolled his eyes, reached over, and turned the volume knob to zero just as the first ad began to play. They both hated radio ads that interrupted their tunes, and always turned off the radio or lowered the volume for a few minutes to be sure the annoyance had passed. Had they left the volume at an audible level, they would have caught the weather update at the end of the commercial break that stated, "This just in for weather: what looked to be a sunny, beautiful weekend may turn a bit nasty with rain, as the forecast for tonight now calls for a 90 percent chance of showers near the 9:00 p.m. mark and may last until mid-day Saturday. Stay tuned in for more updates."

The boys, oblivious to the possible bad weather, paddled to the shoreline that was about a quarter mile from their campsite and began unloading their gear after they had dragged their canoe out of the water and stored it about fifteen feet from the riverbank.

They had worked for about an hour setting up their tent, stacking wood into the firepit, and assembling their cane poles and tackle boxes for catching some dinner. To Jamie and Kyle, this seemed about as close to heaven as two boys could get.

* * *

Approximately three miles upriver from the boy's campsite was the old overpass bridge. It had been around since the 1960s and was still in OK condition for an older bridge. Most of the townspeople were now using the newer bridge about two more miles upriver from the old overpass that was built when the bypass went up about five years ago.

The old overpass was rarely used anymore, but today made for an exception in this case. An old mental asylum in the north end of the state had become rundown and had been closed and condemned by the state. All patients that could be deemed fit for release, or patients that could be cared for well enough by family or nursing homes, were relocated; those that the state doctors deemed mentally unfit to function in public or too much danger to themselves and others were transported around the country to any place that could house and care for them. Old Coney, age fifty, was one of those cases. Diagnosed at age fifteen with severe bipolar disorder and obsessive-compulsive disorder with bouts of demented rage, Coney was discovered in his parent's barn with two smaller kids, a boy and girl, whom he had tied to the wooden support beams. He was discovered before any physical harm could occur to either child, but later had confessed to his therapist at the asylum that his intentions were to torture and murder each kid because they had earlier taunted him on the street and followed him almost all of the way home, calling him names like Crazy Coney. During their search of the barn, police also found the mutilated skeletons and partially rotted carcasses of a few neighborhood dogs and cats that had gone missing over the course of a few years. After analysis and psychiatric testing, doctors had deemed Mr. Coney was too unfit for the public domain, and the state prosecutor sentenced him to life in an asylum under close doctor's supervision.

Coney was the very last patient to leave the asylum before the doors were closed for good. He was to be transported almost two hundred miles south to a secured mental hospital that could accommodate him. That was the plan, and it went smoothly until about a mile up the road from the overpass bridge when Coney's van driver, an older and overweight gentleman in his late sixties, began to feel a tingle that ran up his left arm and had become a crushing pain in his chest by the time he reached the overpass bridge. The driver slumped over and became lifeless as his weight on the steering wheel pulled the van sharply to the left and straight through the old aluminum guard rail that ran along the edge of the bridge. The van plunged some thirty feet down, grill first, before hitting the river and slamming Coney from his seat in the back into the guard cage that separated him from his driver. Coney was able to kick out a side window and escape before the van sank beneath the currents. He was not concerned with the well-being of his driver as he swam to the closest riverbank and lay in the soft dirt to let the dizziness and ringing in his ears subside a bit before trying to stand.

The real earth felt good beneath his feet as he stood. He had forgotten how it felt to stand on anything except tile and concrete flooring. He welcomed the earthy smell of the riverbed and trees around him as he stood on that bank. It would be hours or maybe even a whole day before anyone would suspect him missing when his van didn't arrive at the hospital, and even longer before the van would be found and a search would ensue. Coney knew that, yeah, eventually they would find him, but not for some time, so why not have fun until then—fun like he used to have; fun that got him locked away all of those years ago.

※ ※ ※

Kyle looked up at the sky from his fishing line that had been in the water and untouched for maybe an hour since his last catch. It would be getting dark in about an hour, and he and Jamie still had to clean their catches. Jamie had caught five fish, and Kyle had caught four—it would be plenty for tonight. They cleaned their fish on the bank and made their way back to camp to build a fire.

The sun was just disappearing behind the tree line of pines that populated most of the riverbank as Jamie took the last fillet from the fire and offered it to Kyle, who refused. Both boys were full and ready to relax by the fire for a while before calling it a night. Kyle had cut away two thicker tree limbs while they were fishing and began fashioning them into walking sticks for their exploring trip along the river the next day. The sticks would be flat on one end and sharpened a bit on the other. It was the river, after all, and sometimes you could run into some unfriendly wildlife out there. They had never encountered anything more than a frightened snake or two, but better safe than sorry.

It was around the 9:15 p.m. mark, and both boys were in their sleeping bags inside the tent. They were just about to drift off to sleep when the first drop of rain hit the top of their tent, then another drop and another. The drops soon became a drizzle, which then became a downpour. It wasn't until the water began to fill the bottom of their tent that both boys decided to pack up and head for the boat.

Jamie rolled up the tent and packed it away while Kyle rolled the sleeping bags and packed them in the other supply bag. Things weren't perfectly in order, but they both knew that if the rain was constant, they would be wading through knee-deep water back to the canoe, which didn't sound too fun or safe at night for either boy. With the combination of the now heavy rain and their focus on packing, neither of them noticed the pair of demented eyes that watched them from the heavy brush beyond their campground.

Jamie finished packing the tent first, grabbed a flashlight, and headed for the canoe. His intention was to drop the tent in the canoe at the landing and return to help Kyle finish packing the remaining gear. Kyle watched as Jamie's light became more faint and he got further from the site and closer to the landing, but soon turned his gaze back to his packing.

It seemed about ten minutes had passed since Jamie had left. Kyle had packed the remaining gear and had decided to not wait for Jamie to return but to meet him at the canoe. The remaining gear was a bit heavy for Kyle to carry, but he managed. His mind ran a bit around what would have taken Jamie so long and why he hadn't returned to help finish packing. His mind was suddenly and horribly put to rest as he reached the landing spot. All Kyle could do was stand there and gaze in horror at what he saw. His hand went numb, and his flashlight fell to the already muddy bank of the river.

The canoe had been flipped over and a series of hatchet-blade-sized holes had been chopped all over the belly of their only means of transport back to the landing where they had started. This sight was what originally stopped Kyle in his tracks, but what made him freeze completely was what he saw draped across the now useless and overturned canoe. It was Jamie, lying face down and motionless on the canoe; there were red, blood smeared handprints, about the size of Jamie's hands, all over the canoe bottom where Jamie now lay motionless. This was why Kyle's flashlight now lay in a puddle of mud that filled steadily with rain water. Kyle tried to will himself to step forward and check on his friend, to confirm his fear that his best friend was—he could barely fathom the thought of the word—dead.

Kyle managed the mental strength to reach down and pick up his light and also his walking stick that he had carved earlier that day. These were his only means of any kind of protection, as Jamie had taken both the hatchet and the machete with him to the canoe. The chill bumps that now ran up Kyle's neck and that dry taste in his mouth both told him that whoever had done this to his friend, most likely had both in their possession now. Each foot now seemed to weigh a hundred pounds as he stepped closer to Jamie's body, and he almost once again froze in place and dropped his light as its beam cut through the rain and landed on his friend's face. It was the hatchet that had destroyed the bottom of their canoe, but it was the machete at the hands of some monster that had taken his friend from him. All at once, fear, adrenaline, and disgust hit Kyle so hard, that all he could do was grab his stomach to double over and let everything that he had eaten that day make its way back up from out of his gut and onto the muddy earth. There were barely a few seconds to recover from the wrenching in his gut and the sour taste in his mouth. Kyle had no chance to vomit again when he stood upright, as a heavy hand had forcefully grabbed all of the hair on the top of his head and snatched him about three feet backward. He banged into a solid figure dressed in a mud-stained set of mental hospital scrubs. The next series of events happened in such a blur that Kyle could only remember what transpired after he was in the fast moving river and treading as best he could to stay above water.

He remembered the pain in his scalp from being snatched backward by his hair. He was fairly sure there'd been a great deal of hair pulled out. He remembered almost having the wind knocked from his lungs as his back slammed solidly into Coney's chest and abdomen, and he could feel the hot and heavy breath on his left ear as the cold metal of a machete blade touched the right side of his neck.

The detail of how he was still alive had become clear only now as he felt something heavily bump into his back. Kyle jerked in fear at first with the thought that this evil man had jumped in behind him and had caught up with him to finish the job, but the heavy hit had come from a much-needed object—a big log had fallen into the river and been pulled toward him by the river's currant. Kyle grabbed onto the debris with all of his strength, and the sharp pain from a four-inch cut that started above his chest and ended on the back of his right shoulder made his mind become a bit more clear now as to how he was still alive. He rested his arms and legs to let the floating log do the work of carrying him back to his original landing in the darkness.

Coney's hand had let go of Kyle's scalp and made its way to the back of his neck, forming a painful vice grip that would have put Kyle on his knees if he had not been held upright by Coney himself. Coney sadistically laid the blade of the machete on Kyle's right shoulder with the dull edge against Kyle's neck, almost as if to toy with him a bit before sending him to join his face-down friend on the canoe. Kyle felt the machete blade on his neck and panicked. Not knowing which edge was touching his neck; he reacted without thinking and plunged the sharpened end of his walking stick into what felt like Coney's side. As Coney staggered backward in pain, the sharp edge of the blade dragged across the top of Kyle's chest and shoulder, sending a stinging pain into his chest and shoulder muscles. He first fell to his hands and knees in the mud as Coney staggered backward and tripped over one of the camping packs that had been dropped. Coney lay there for a few seconds, growling and moaning in pain as he tried to remove the sharp stick from his abdomen. Kyle, taking advantage of this much-needed distraction, did all that he could think to do: He grabbed his light and ran as fast as he could across the muddy riverbank. He fell into the even faster-moving current, hoping the darkness and heavy rain would give him enough cover to escape and safely float back to where Jamie's dad had dropped them off. He switched off his flashlight and half treaded water and half floated as the current took him toward safety.

Coney had lain in pain for what seemed like thirty seconds before attempting to remove the stick from his gut. He'd cried and growled in anger as the stick pulled past the muscle. It felt like his abdomen was on fire as he stood to his feet just in time to see Kyle's flashlight go out as the current swept him away. It wasn't anger that filled him as he followed suit and plunged into the current about one hundred yards behind Kyle. It was a pure and sadistic pleasure that filled his mind. He had dropped the machete when he had fallen and now was in complete darkness, but it made no difference to Coney. He was happy enough to finish his new victim with his bare hands. He never allowed himself to float too close to Kyle as he treaded slowly behind and waited for that flashlight to turn back on.

Kyle was almost blind in the darkness as he floated. He didn't want to risk turning on the light too much, as he wasn't sure if Coney was dead or alive or if he had followed him into the river. His sight slowly adjusted to the darkness, and he could make out various shapes along the riverbank, like trees or bigger rocks that lay along the bank line. Fear slowly began to creep into his mind that maybe he had drifted past his landing in the darkness. He knew it was about five miles until the next landing, and maybe he would miss that in the darkness. But his fear was put to rest as a small bit of moonlight reflected off a few of the bigger rocks that lined each side of the boat landing. He clung onto the log and treaded with his good arm as he kicked hard with his feet. His aim was a bit off due to his injury and exhaustion—he came to shore at some of the bigger rocks a few feet past the concrete landing ramp, but he was happy enough just the same to be closer to safety. He gave no bother to the rocks that slightly cut his hands and knees as he crawled from the river and collapsed onto his stomach. He rolled over onto his back and rested the back of his head on one of the bigger rocks. Thank God it was smooth at least. His attempt to take a deep, relieving breath of the night air was cut very short as a big pair of hands came out of the darkness and clamped around his throat.

Coney's sight had also adjusted to the darkness as he floated behind Kyle. He had sighted the landing before Kyle, and had begun to quietly close the gap between them. He had been a few feet behind as he'd watched his prey crawl slowly onto the rocks and out of the water. His original thought was to jump on the kid and smash his face into the rocks as he lay face down, but as Coney stood slowly to his feet, the pain in his stomach caused him to pause and wince just a bit and his window was missed, as Kyle had rolled onto his back. Coney didn't waste another second this time. He took about five big paces and leaped onto Kyle's formerly prone figure.

Coney's hands made contact as he wrapped his thick fingers around the twelve-year-old's esophagus and squeezed, not enough to kill right away, but enough to drain any fight that his victim might exhibit. Just as the light was about to go out in Kyle's eyes, as an extra precaution, Coney lifted Kyle's head up about six inches from the rock behind his head and returned it back to its former resting place with force. Coney let go of his grip as he watched his victim begin to fade into unconsciousness. He felt around a bit on the rocks until he found a bigger stone that fit into his hands almost perfectly. Coney took the big rock in both of his hands and raised it above his victim's head. A euphoric smile spread across his face.

Kyle had felt nothing but a sting in his lungs as the hands had squeezed tight around his throat. Every attempted breath had yielded nothing but pain. He could make out the evil pleasure in Coney's eyes as his vision began getting dark and his ears began ringing, which intensified tenfold when he felt the back of his head strike something hard and unforgiving. The last thing he recalled before the darkness was the smiling face of his aggressor. A big rock was being held above his face. He only hoped to fade out quickly before Coney and his rock did their damage. The blackness did come before the rock could strike its mark.

※ ※ ※

Kyle felt nothing for a brief moment—nothing that is until a palm struck his face a few times. Was Coney trying to wake him? Did this sick monster want him awake when he finished him off? But it wasn't Coney's hand that had struck his face. It was the hand of the game warden that snapped Kyle awake. The next few hours were foggy with images after he was awakened: the game warden's muffled voice trying to keep him conscious because of his possible concussion, two local police officers covering Coney's lifeless body, which now had bullet holes in the chest thanks to one of the officers and his .38 revolver, and finally the oxygen mask being placed over Kyle's face to aid a bit in his breathing.

The game warden and two local police officers had been sent with a boat to search the river area when a patrol car had passed the smashed guardrail on the overpass and reported a possible accident. They had arrived at the landing to put their boat in the river, and they'd seen Coney on top of Kyle with the rock raised above his head. After a loud and unheeded warning to drop the rock, one of the officers had fired several shots into Coney, who had then fallen lifeless on top of an unconscious Kyle as the rock had dropped from Coney's hands and fallen behind him. The medical professionals had arrived shortly after and had begun to carefully place Kyle on a gurney and secure his neck.

Kyle watched to the side as the black bag was zipped up around Coney's corpse. He also watched as a boat pulled onto the landing pad from the river and two officers climbed out carrying a smaller black body bag that had been zipped up. Tears escaped from Kyle's tired eyes, as he knew what its contents were.

✲ ✲ ✲

It was 2:55 p.m. on an early summer day in 1991, and the last five minutes of Kyle's school day seemed to take no time at all to pass by as Kyle stared steadily down at his empty desktop. Kyle hadn't noticed the time at all and had to be broken from his gaze by his teacher's voice to let him know it was time to go home and enjoy his summer. His only thought was that September wouldn't arrive fast enough.

His dad was waiting just outside his classroom door to walk him to their car—this was a required thing from Kyle now to feel safe. He reached up to rub the scar on his right shoulder after he buckled his seat belt, and his dad drove them toward home.

PART 2
FANTASY

SOMEHOW

Somehow, some way,
I can make it through this day.
Somehow, some way,
I am certain I will be OK.
Somehow, some way,
I can soon be in your arms one day.
Somehow, some way,
I can kiss your lips and softly say.
Somehow, some way,
I do not have to go away.
Somehow, some way…

PATH OF THE SUN

There once was a young brave that stood on the East Hill every morning to greet the Great Sun as it rose. Every morning the young brave would ask of the wise Sun, "Oh, Great Sun, you see the entire world every day and surely are very wise because of the many things you have seen. Will you please share with me your wisdom, so that I may be as wise as you are?"

Finally, after growing tired of the young brave's relentless request, the Great Sun agreed. "Tomorrow morning follow me in my path across the sky, young brave, and if you catch me at my final resting place on the West Mountain before I sleep, I will enlighten you as to what is true wisdom."

The next morning the young brave anxiously awaited the Great Sun's awakening, and just as the Great Sun arose, the young brave began his chase as fast as he could run. A few hours into his journey, he passed the teepee of Old Widow, who called to him as he passed. "You look hungry, young brave. If you are kind enough to bring me the heavy timbers for my fire, I will cook for you the finest fry bread in the plains."

But the young brave would not give in to the temptation of Old Widow, even though his stomach growled deeply with hunger. He only replied, "No, Old Widow, I must catch the Great Sun before he sleeps, so that I may know true wisdom." So onward the young brave ran, proud of himself for staying the course and not giving in to temptation.

The brave continued running for what seemed like half the day. Even though he was a healthy young brave, fatigue was beginning to set in, and he began to grow weary, when he passed yet another teepee. This was the teepee of Lovely Squaw, the most beautiful woman of the hills. Lovely Squaw called out to the young brave, "Young brave, you are very strong and handsome, and I am quite lonely here alone. Please, come join me. You can share my home, and we can have a good life together. You are a fine brave, and I would promise to be a fine wife for you."

The young brave slowed a bit, but only for a moment. Lovely Squaw was just that indeed, and he entertained just for a moment what a life with her would be like. But once again, he pushed the temptation from his mind and began now to run at even a faster pace than when he'd begun his chase. He scolded himself for almost giving in to the temptation of Lovely Squaw, but continued his chase nonetheless.

As many more hours passed, the young brave could now see the West Mountain in the distance and began to run even faster in worry of not catching the Great Sun before he slept. But as he picked up speed, he felt a crushing pain in his heart that felt hot like fire.

Just before reaching the base of the West Mountain, the young brave passed the talking Old Oak that stood watch over the Young River. As the young brave passed, the Old Oak called to him. "Brave, you look so tired. I know your journey of chasing the Great Sun has not been an easy one. It is very hot this close to the Great Sun's resting place. Won't you rest beneath my shade and drink from Young River. You can sleep here and meet the Great Sun tomorrow as he passes.

The brave could almost taste the cold water from Young River on his lips and could already feel the shade of the Old Oak .But he pushed these from his mind despite the burning pain in his chest and the dry cough that now escaped his lips as he ran.

He was proud of himself once again for resisting temptation from his journey, and to his surprise, he arrived at the West Mountain a few moments ahead of the Great Sun. As the Great Sun approached him, the young brave fell to his knees from exhaustion and gripped his chest as he spoke, "Great Sun, I, the young brave, have caught you before you sleep. Now, tell me of wisdom as you have promised.

The Great Sun replied, "Young brave, I see before me no young brave at all. I only see a tired old man. You see, old brave, this journey, although had only seemed to you as one day, has taken fifty summers. Because you remained so focused on your destination, you lost concept of time and are now a tired old brave."

Yet still, the now old brave was relentless. "You still made a promise of wisdom, and I demand you keep it!

The Great Sun answered with this: "There is no more wisdom for me to show you that the path I had laid out for you would have shown you. I saw the same things every day along my path and only wished that even one of these things would be successful in tempting you from your overeager journey. First I tried to share with you the wisdom that is reward for helping others that cannot help themselves; second was the wisdom to realize the true value from the love and care of a woman; and third was the wisdom to love and care for yourself, despite your drive toward a goal. You are now dying, old brave; but fear not, your diligence will not go completely unrewarded. You will not die a normal death, but will join me in the sky; but not as my equal. You will always journey a day behind me on my path, seeing in nighttime what I have seen in daytime. I will always be the Great Sun with no equal in wisdom. You will only shine with a reflection of my great wisdom, but you will cease to be known as young or old brave and will forever be known as Brother Moon.

WORKING HANDS

There once was a Great Chief of the South Lands. He was blessed five times over with daughters. Each daughter was blessed with a different gift that benefited the chief and his entire tribe in some way.

Singing Bird was the youngest of the five. Singing Bird was not only beautiful, but also had the gift to make music with her voice or with her many flutes that were carved by hand.

Calming Touch, who was only one year older than Singing Bird, also had tremendous beauty, and had the ability to heal the soreness from her father's bones and muscles, that came from his days of labor or hunting, just from her touch and the use of heated stones.

Painted Heart, who was just one year older than Calming Touch, was seen by the young braves as the loveliest of the Great Chief's five daughters. She had great gifts to create the most beautiful of cave paintings, and was responsible for painting the faces of the young braves and elders for celebrations and religious ceremonies.

Mending Mind was just one year older than Painted Heart, and was the most logical of the five daughters. She could not only repair and sew together clothes and teepees for the entire village, but she was also a skilled problem solver because of her sharp mind and logic.

Then there was Working Hands. She was the eldest and most plain of the chief's five daughters, although still very beautiful like her four younger siblings. She possessed only the skill of hard work and diligence. She was not only the oldest daughter, but also one of the first members of the chief's tribe, as she was born to her parents as they were traveling and working alone, before her father's rise to leadership. This meant that from the day she was able, she was working beside her father and mother in the fields for crop gathering or in the forest for hunting. These many years of laboring for her father and her tribe had taken its toll on her hands—they became large, scarred, and calloused. She was often teased by the young braves or her sisters about her large hands, but never relented in her work or took the teasing to heart. If there was hard work to be done, there you would find Working Hands.

There came one day, from the clouds, a messenger bird with an important message to the Great Chief. "Great Chief of the South Lands, I am the messenger bird of the Sun Chief in the sky. The Sun Chief has become old and very sick, and his burning light that gives light and warmth to all of the lands will soon fade forever unless he can pass his power to his son. His son is incomplete and must find a wife in order to become complete to continue on in his father's stead. The Sun Chief has chosen your tribe from which his son is to find a wife, because your tribe is the most prosperous of all of the tribes of the lands. Can you accommodate the Sun Chief's wishes for the sake of all of the lands?"

The Great Chief happily answered, "I have but five daughters here in my tribe who are of age to marry. I will take council with my lovely daughters and can have your answer before day's end."

The messenger bird waited while the Great Chief met with his daughters. Each daughter agreed to help and would be happy to take the side of the new Great Sun Chief if chosen.

One week later there was to be a great ceremony of choice at the tribe's sacred grounds, for this was the place where the Great Sun Chief's heir would ascend from the sky lands and choose, not only his bride, but the one to make him complete enough to give light and warmth to all of the lands below. Each daughter prepared herself to offer the services of their gifts to the future Sun Chief. In doing so, their duties to the tribe were somewhat neglected—this was an important occasion, and they each wanted to impress the new Sun Chief. Each daughter, except for Working Hands, that is, who diligently tended to her duties of her tribe. She also loved her sisters so much and was so certain that one of them would certainly be chosen for their gifts and beauty that she even helped them to complete their missed duties in order for them to prepare themselves for the ceremony of choice.

Just mere hours before the new Sun Chief's dissension from the clouds, the Great Chief noticed that all of his daughters were waiting inside the sacred circle except for his eldest daughter, Working Hands. As he searched for her, he found her in the fields gathering the last of the tribe's daily harvested corn. "Daughter, you are not at the ceremony. You must hurry to greet the new Sun Chief as he arrives."

"I know father," she answered. "But this is the last of today's harvest. If I leave it here, it could be taken by birds or become rancid, and that would be a great loss to our tribe. The new Sun Chief still has my younger sisters to choose from. Surely one of their great gifts will be enough to make him complete."

The Great Chief smiled as he bent and kissed his daughter on the forehead. "My eldest daughter and my first great creation, you are always working. I am a proud man to have five great daughters, and it all began with you, my lovely Working Hands. I will help you finish so that you may take your place inside the circle with your sisters."

Working Hands had just stepped into the circle of choice as the future Sun Chief appeared from the sky and landed in the center of the circle. Although he was young, he was very wise for his age. He greeted each of the daughters as he turned inside of the circle. "I am aware that you are all very gifted and can see that each one of you is very beautiful."

Working Hands lowered her head a bit as the future Sun Chief spoke of beauty. She had no time to prepare herself and thought herself very plain.

The young chief spoke again. "I can see that you have all prepared yourselves by using your special talents, and although this is very flattering, it will not be necessary regarding my choice. All I will ask of each of you is that you raise your right hand with your palms pressed toward me.

As odd as this sounded, each of the daughters did what was requested of them. The future chief approached Singing Bird first, as she was the youngest. As he reached her, he simply placed the palm of his left hand against the palm of her right hand. As their palms touched, he noticed his own hand was much larger than Signing Birds. He paused for a moment and then spoke. "You are very beautiful and talented. I have heard many of your songs up in the sky. But I am sorry. You cannot be the one to make me complete." Singing Bird stepped from the circle and joined her father.

The future chief then approached Calming Touch and placed his left palm to her right palm. As before, his very large hand engulfed hers as it had her younger sister's. He spoke once more. "You are very beautiful, and I have watched many days as your touch has helped to heal the tired and weary of you tribe. This is a great gift, but I am sorry. You cannot be the one that completes me." Calming Touch left the circle and joined her father and sister.

The chief and his daughters all found the future chief's method to be very odd but kept their silence as he made his way to Painted Heart. He once more pressed his left palm to her right palm. Her fingertip almost matched his in length. "You are the most gifted painter that I have ever seen, and many of my father's clouds and skylines are based on your paintings." The chief and other sisters thought surely that the future chief had made his choice. To their surprise, he said, "I am sorry, but you cannot be the one that completes me." As her sister before her, she joined her father outside of the circle.

The future chief then stood in front of Mending Mind, and just like the three times previous, placed his left palm to her right. Mending Mind was of a small build, and her entire palm barely filled the center of the future chief's hand. He again spoke. "Mending Mind, you are not only the wisest of you sisters, but you are the wisest person of all of the tribe lands. You will do many amazing works for your people with your mind and will one day lead them to prosperity. But I, again, am sorry. You are not the one to complete me."

Mending Mind left the circle and joined her father.

Working Hands now hung her head lower and became very nervous as she thought to herself, "I am the last. He surely cannot choose me. My tribe may be disgraced because the Great Sun Chief had chosen my father's tribe for a proper bride to complete the future Sun Chief." She lowered her hand from embarrassment. The future chief had made his decision just from touching the other's hands. "He surely will not find what he needs with my very large and scarred hands," she thought to herself.

The future chief approached Working Hands. "Working Hands is your name, correct?"

"Yes it is," she answered.

"Will you do me the honor of presenting your right palm?"

After a moment of doubt, she raised her right palm and pushed it in the future chief's direction as he met her palm with his. When their palms touched, he immediately noticed that her calloused fingertips extended beyond his by almost half an inch. She awaited the previous response received by her sisters, but got only another question from the young man as he smirked a bit at their touching hands.

"Would you be so kind as to now raise your left palm, Working Hands?"

She obliged and slowly raised her left palm to the same height as her right. He placed his right palm into her left and smiled a bit at his discovery. His right fingers extended beyond her left fingers in length. By this time, Working Hands, her sisters, and her father were all a bit confused, but even more so at the future chief's next question.

"Is your right hand your strong hand?"

"Yes," she replied.

He smiled once more and spoke again. "Mine also."

There were a few more moments of silence before the future chief broke it. "Working Hands, I watched daily as you worked without thought of yourself but only for the good of first your father, mother, and sisters, and then for your tribe. But I am sorry…that you will have to say goodbye to them if it is your wish to join me in the sky, as you are the one to complete me in my place as the Great Sun Chief."

Working Hands stood for a moment in disbelief at the future chief's decision. The young chief noticed her disbelief and offered his explanation to quell her confusion.

"Your right hand, which is your strong hand, is larger than my left hand, which is my weak hand. This means that you can be strong when and where I am weak. In turn, my right hand, which is my strong hand, is larger than your left hand, which is your weak hand. That means that I can be strong where you are weak. We form a complete balance, and this means you can make me complete. You see, Working Hands, many years ago, my father, the Great Sun Chief, was joined by a young brave in the sky. This brave became known as Brother Moon. Brother Moon sometimes becomes very jealous of my father and seeks to block my father's light from the tribes of the South Lands. Your people have come to know this as the eclipse. It is during this time that my father becomes very weak, and if not for the aid of my very strong mother, he would lose his place in the sky to Brother Moon—who always seeks to take my father's place by chasing father across the skies—and all of the tribes of the South Lands would forever be in darkness and void of warmth."

After hearing the future chief's explanation, Working Hands made the difficult decision to bid farewell to her tribe and family, and joined the new Great Sun Chief in the sky.

The next morning, Working Hands and the new Sun Chief met inside of the circle of choosing to ascend together into the sky. The new Great Sun Chief couldn't help but notice his bride's sadness to leave her family and tribe, so he offered her a gift to honor her work and sacrifice.

"It is a sad thing to leave your home and all that you know. For your great sacrifice and work, I wish to grant blessings to you and your family's tribe. Name anything you wish, and I can grant it for you, Working Hands."

Working hands thought for a moment and then gave only three requests. "First, I will always be sad to leave my home, and I will cry many tears. Can you see that these tears fall as rain onto the South Lands to supply water to crops, rivers, and lakes, so that no tribe will ever face drought? Second, as I have spent many years working in the fields to tend crops for my tribe, I have noticed that your father was always giving of his warmth and light to make our crops grow. But sometimes this could also cause great exhaustion and even burns to the skin of the field-workers below. Will you bless me with the ability to shade my people occasionally from your powerful rays so that they may take ease and rest? My last wish it a bit difficult to figure. If you can grant it, my new husband, it would be a way to show my family how much I love and miss them, but I cannot think of a strong enough way to express this to them."

The new Sun Chief thought for a few moments of how to grant these three unselfish wishes. "Even now, Working Hands, you think only of others.I have always found this to be an admirable trait as I looked down on you from my father's sky. I will grant your first wish that your tears replenish the tribes of the South Lands with water, and I shall call it rain.I will grant your second wish to cover your family and tribe from my heat at times, and I shall call it clouds, and from these clouds, at times when you are sad, your tears will fall. As far as your last wish of your symbol of love to your home and family that you will miss, after your tears of rain have fallen, I will shine my powerful light through them, and this point in the sky will be cascaded with many beautiful colors.This symbol of love to your family shall be called a rainbow. And also, to reward your further unselfish wishes and sacrifice, I shall grant you a gift of my choosing, my new bride.When the days comes that your father, mother, sisters, and fellow tribe members cannot continue on in the South Lands, they will not be buried into the earth like the other tribe peoples of the South Lands.They will join you here in the sky, and they will, from then on, be known as stars, as they will light the night skies with great beauty while you and I take our rest.This shall be our cycle from this day forward until the day that a new Great Sun Chief is chosen to replace us in the great big sky.

HARRY AND THE SUN FAIRY

Little Harry loved playing outside. It was his absolute favorite thing to do after school and on the weekends. He was so excited on this particular Saturday morning because it had rained all the night before, and the only thing better than playing outside was playing outside after it rained. He loved jumping in all the puddles while walking with his mom or his grandma from his house and the playground. Harry made sure to splash every single puddle without missing a single one. Sometimes he would get his mom or grandma wet or muddy by mistake and be in a little trouble about it. This didn't worry him at the moment as he ran around his apartment shouting, "Let's go, Mamma! Let's go, Grandma!" It took both his mom and grandma working together to get him to sit still long enough to put on his raincoat and boots.

As Harry stood at the door and waited impatiently to go outside, his mom looked down to him and said something that did not make him happy at all.

"Now, Harry, Mom wants to remain clean today. So we will walk to the playground and play, but there will be no puddle splashing today."

Harry was not happy at all to hear this, but still hung his head and mumbled a single "OK" to let his mom know that he understood. Once they were in agreement, out the door and off to the park they went. Little did he know, this was not going to be a normal day at the playground—not at all.

Harry saw at least twenty puddles between his house and the playground, and as much as he wanted to splash each one, he remembered his mom's words and walked by each puddle without even stepping one foot in a single puddle. He and his mom arrived at the playground, and his mom took a seat on the bench just outside of the playground fence. He stood beside her until she was seated.

"Well," she said, "go on. And remember, no splashing Mom's jeans or shoes, please."

Harry nodded in agreement and ran in the direction of the slides and monkey bars.

Harry climbed up the stairs of the jungle gym and sat at the top of the tallest slide. This was Harry's favorite slide on the playground because it was the tallest and the stairs that led to the top of the slide were shaped like a rocket ship. He loved standing at the top and looking out over the playground before sliding down as fast as he could. He looked once at his mom as she sat on the park bench, reading her book. He sat down on the slide and rocked back and forth a few times to build up as much speed as he could so that he could slide down really fast. He was just about to let go when a small voice cried out from behind him, "I wouldn't do that if I were you, boy."

Harry grabbed a bar over his head to stop himself from sliding down the slide. "Who said that?" he asked as he turned around to look. He hadn't seen any other kids on the entire playground when he'd arrived, and this voice had caught him completely by surprise.

"I did!" answered a small voice from overhead.

Harry looked up, and to his surprise, he saw a small figure hanging from the ceiling of the rocketship slide. Harry stared in surprise for a few seconds before speaking to the small creature. "What are you?"

The small creature dropped down from the ceiling and landed on Harry's knee as Harry sat at the top of the slide. "Hello," the little creature said. "I'm a sun fairy."

"What's a sun fairy?" asked Harry.

"I use my magic staff to bring the sun out after it rains or snows, but I dropped my staff at the bottom of this slide, and now I can't get it, and if I don't point my staff at the sky, it will remain cloudy and rainy forever."

"Well, why don't you climb down and get your staff?" Harry asked.

"I can't," replied the little creature. "You see… um, I'm sorry. What is your name, boy?"

"Oh," replied Harry. " My name is Harry. What is your name, little fairy?"

"I don't know my name. We sun fairies don't have names."

Harry thought for a moment. "Can I call you Sunny, since you are responsible for making the sun come out?"

The fairy scratched his head for a moment and then smiled. "I've never had a name before. I like Sunny! Pleased to meet you, Harry! My name is Sunny, and as I was saying before, I dropped my magic staff just below this very slide that we sit on now. I was walking through this playground, and I was just about to point my staff up to the sky when three very nasty mud goblins pushed me down, and I dropped my stick. Have you ever seen a mud goblin, Harry?"

Harry twisted his mouth a bit in confusion and shook his head.

"Well, Harry, just as sun fairies bring the sun, mud goblins bring the rain. But they do not like sharing the sky one little bit, so they do what they can to keep it cloudy and rainy. Mud goblins love when it's cloudy and wet outside. You most likely haven't seen one before because they loved hiding in the mud and puddles that happen after it rains. Three of them were soaking in the rain puddles on this playground and got angry at me when they saw me about to bring out the sun. Mud goblins are mean bullies in my world. There isn't much that we sun fairies can do against them because they are also three times our size."

Harry thought for a moment and then asked, "Do you want me to help you get your staff back, Sunny?"

"That's very brave of you, Harry, but I'm afraid it will not be easy. The only way to stop a mud goblin is to jump on its head and squash it flat. Plus humans can't see mud goblins, so how will you know where they are to jump on them?"

Harry propped his chin on his head and thought hard.

"I have it!" Harry shouted. "I can't see them, but you can, Sunny. You can ride on my shoulders as I slide down, and when you see a mud goblin in front of me, tell me when to jump. That way, they can't reach you. Once we've squashed them all, we can find your magic staff."

"Hmm," Sunny said aloud. "It will be tricky, but it could work, and I really have to get that sun out from behind the clouds."

Harry turned back around and pointed his legs down the slide. Sunny hopped up onto Harry's shoulders and wrapped each of his legs around Harry's neck as he spoke to Harry. "Good luck, Harry!"

"Don't mention it," Harry replied as he reached up and shook Sunny's hand.

Down the slide they went. *Whoosh!* Harry felt the wind in his hair as he went sliding. He had never slid this fast before in his life.

They were about halfway down the slide when Sunny shouted into his ear, "Oh no! Harry, there's one at the base of the slide in the puddle! Get ready to jump, Harry!"

They were near the base of the slide when Harry jumped to his feet and began running.

"Now, Harry! Jump!" yelled Sunny.

Harry leaped from the base of the slide and jumped as high and fast into the air as he could. He landed directly in the middle of the puddle with a great *splash* then a *squash* onto the mud goblin's head, squashing it completely flat and also splashing water in every direction.

"We got one! Great job, Harry!" yelled Sunny.

Harry's mom looked up in sheer surprise and yelled herself. "Harry! What did I say?"

Harry paused for a moment, completely embarrassed. He had forgotten his promise to his mom. His distraction only lasted for a second, as Sunny spoke into his ear. "Harry, look out!"

Harry felt a pain in the toe on his right foot and yelped a bit. "Ouch! Sunny, what was that?"

"That was a mud goblin, Harry. They're trying to stomp your toes so that you cannot jump anymore. There are only two more left, Harry."

Sunny looked around the playground and quickly spotted the next mud goblin. "There, Harry! Hiding in the puddle, just below the end of the monkey bars."

Harry turned and ran toward the puddle, but Sunny warned him just before reaching the bars at the opposite end of the puddle. "Look out, Harry! The one that stomped your toe is right at the other end of the bars. Looks like he will try to trip you. How will you get to the other side?"

Harry thought and then replied, "Let me know when I'm close to the toe stomper."

Sunny knew immediately what Harry was thinking and yelled just as the toe stomper raised his foot to stomp Harry's toes. "Now, Harry!"

Harry jumped over the stomper and grabbed the first rung of the monkey bars. He quickly handwalked the rungs at what seemed like the speed of light and jumped just as he got to the end. *Splash… squash*—another one squashed. Only one goblin left.

"Where's that toe stomper, Sunny? Do you see him anywhere?"

Sunny looked steadily around the playground and saw the last mud goblin, the toe stomper, but he didn't like what he was about to tell Harry. "Harry, I found the last one, and you're not going to like this at all."

"What's wrong, Sunny?" Harry asked.

"Well…" Sunny hesitated. "The good news is, I found him. The bad news is, he has my magic staff."

"Ok," Harry answered. "Let's go get it."

Sunny responded reluctantly. "The other bad news is that he just hid in a puddle that's right beside that lady there." Sunny pointed to Harry's mom.

Harry's stomach dropped a bit as he spoke to Sunny. "Sunny, promise me one thing?"

"Anything, brave sir," Sunny replied.

"Make sure it's extra sunny for an extra-long time when we get that staff back. It may be a while before I'm allowed out to enjoy a sunny day."

"It's a promise, Harry the Mud Goblin Slayer."

Harry's mom had looked up and rolled her eyes as she heard Harry splash, yet again, into a second puddle. "That hard headed boy." She mumbled to herself as she looked back down to her book. "I'll be cleaning his boots and drying his socks again… ugh."

She was again focused on her book; so focused that she didn't notice her own son running like the wind in her direction. She paused to check on Harry just in time to see the boy leaping into the air in her direction. The confused look on her face turned quickly to fear as her gaze shifted from Harry to the enormous, muddy-water-filled puddle that was on the ground beside her bench.

As the leap happened, seemingly in slow motion, one single word was able to escape her lips. "Nooooooooo!" she yelled, but it was clearly too late. Harry was already in the air when he realized that maybe he had been running too fast to land safely in the puddle. His feet shot wildly out in front of him just before he landed, bottom first in the puddle beside his mom.

Splaaaaash—water and mud exploded from the puddle, followed by a great big *squaaaaash* as the last mud goblin squashed flat beneath Harry's bottom. The magic staff flew into the air as Sunny leaped from Harry's shoulders and grabbed the staff out of the air.

Harry sat in the mud puddle for a few seconds, struggling to breath, as the landing had knocked the wind from Harry's lungs. He shook the dizziness from his head just in time to see yet another mud goblin storming in his direction. This one was bigger and meaner looking than the other three. Harry closed his eyes and waited for the worst. Then the mud goblin spoke in a voice that sounded very familiar.

"Harry! Boy, what were you thinking?"

Harry realized that it wasn't a mud goblin at all. It was his very own mother, who had been covered in muddy water in Harry's last splash down. Judging by the anger on her face, he would have preferred it to be a mud goblin.

His mom grabbed his arm and snatched him from the puddle. "We're going home this instant!

You, young man, can forget any outside playtime for the next month! You've ruined my shoes, clothes, and library book, all which are coming out of your weekly allowance."

Harry smiled a bit as he hung his head. A small voice, unheard by his mother, whispered into his ear, "Thank you, Harry the Mud Goblin Slayer."

Harry walked toward home in his mother's grasp as she scolded him further. The sun slowly began breaking through the clouds behind them.

www.ingramcontent.com/pod-product-compliance
Lightning Source LLC
LaVergne TN
LVHW092057060526
838201LV00047B/1440